OUR PEOPLE

For my father—Howard L. Shelf
with love

—A.S.M

In memory of my mother,
Vera Ellen Bryant,
who made this book possible

—M.B.

OUR PEOPLE

by **Angela Shelf Medearis**

illustrated by **Michael Bryant**

GINGHAM DOG
PRESS

Columbus, Ohio

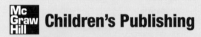

Children's Publishing

Text © 1994 Angela Shelf Medearis
Illustrations © 1994 Michael Bryant
Cover Illustrations © 1994 Michael Bryant

This edition published in the United States of America in 2002 by
Gingham Dog Press,
an imprint of McGraw-Hill Children's Publishing,
a Division of The McGraw-Hill Companies
8787 Orion Place
Columbus, Ohio 43240-4027

www.MHkids.com

Library of Congress Cataloging-in-Publication Data

Medearis, Angela Shelf, 1956–
        Our people / Angela Shelf Medearis; illustrated by Michael Bryant
            p. cm.
        Summary: Parent and child discuss their African-American heritage and the contributions made to civilization by their people.
        ISBN 1-57768-440-0 (HC)
            1. African Americans—History—Juvenile literature. [1. African Americans—History.] I. Bryant, Michael, ill. II. Title.

        E185 .M383 2003
        973'.0496073—dc21   2002033846

Printed in The United States of America.

1-57768-440-0

1 2 3 4 5 6 7 8 9 10 PHXBK 09 08 07 06 05 04 03 02

A Note to Readers from the Author

I wrote *OUR PEOPLE* to introduce African-American history to young children. Each page explores a different accomplishment of African Americans, from building the pyramids to traveling in outer space. My hope is that my account of the various accomplishments of African Americans will fuel dialogue and lead children to further inquiry.

The first African Americans came to America as explorers. In 1492, Pedro Alonzo Nino navigated for Christopher Columbus on his explorations of America. In 1513, Nuflio de Olan sailed with Balboa when he discovered the Pacific Ocean. And, from 1528–1538, Estavanico, or Little Stephen as he was sometimes called, traveled with Spanish explorer Cabeza de Vaca. Estavanico is one of the most famous African explorers. He was de Vaca's servant and accompanied him when he led a 600-member expedition to search for land and gold in Florida and Mexico.

Unfortunately, most African Americans did not come to explore America. Most came as slaves. Slave traders transported millions of African Americans to America before slavery ended in 1865. Of these, many African Americans worked hard to abolish slavery. Frederick Douglass, an escaped slave, became a successful journalist and antislavery leader. William Still used his home as a station on the Underground Railroad, a network of safe hiding places for runaway slaves. Harriet Tubman led slaves to freedom via the Underground Railroad, and Sojourner Truth became a successful anti-slavery speaker.

After the Civil War, African Americans started new lives as free men and women. Some moved west and became farmers and cowboys. One of those was Bill Pickett, a well-known cowboy. He invented a technique of wrestling cattle called "bulldogging," which involved biting the upper lip of a steer and pulling it to the ground on top of him. Even though his technique became popular, it is illegal today. In my own family, my mother's people, the Davis family, moved to Oklahoma and Kansas to become farmers.

Not only were African Americans pioneers in the West, they were pioneers in science. Garrett A. Morgan invented the stoplight. Lewis Latimer invented the electrified filament in light bulbs. Dr. George Washington Carver experimented on peanuts, sweet potatoes, and soybeans, discovering hundreds of industrial uses for them. Dr. Charles Drew helped establish blood banks. And in 1992, Jerretta Jemison blasted off into space to become the first African-American female astronaut.

It is my sincere hope that OUR PEOPLE is more than a celebration of African-American history. Indeed, I see it as a celebration of the human spirit. I want it to open the imaginations of young children to the distinguished past, the exciting present, and the boundless future that lies ahead of them.

–Angela Shelf Medearis

Daddy says our people built the pyramids.

I wish I could have been there. I would have helped them with the plans.

Daddy says our people were kings and queens in Africa. He says some of our people were poets and mathematicians, and some were artists who carved beautiful statues.

I wish I could have been there. I would have been sitting on a throne. Or maybe I would have been an artist.

Daddy says our people traveled across the ocean with Christopher Columbus and explored America with Balboa, Ponce de Leon, and Lewis and Clark.

I wish I could have explored new worlds with them.

Daddy says our people suffered under slavery, but men and women like Frederick Douglass, William Still, Harriet Tubman, and Sojourner Truth led our people to freedom.

I wish I could have been there. I would have led my people to freedom too.

Daddy says our people came out of slavery full of hope, so they could become anything they wanted to be. Some became politicians, some started businesses, and some became teachers and doctors.

I wish I could have been there. I would have gone out West too.

Daddy says that our people created inventions that are still used today. He says that every time we stop at a stoplight or change a light bulb we're using something our people have invented. He says that Garrett A. Morgan, Lewis Latimer, Dr. George Washington Carver, and Dr. Charles Drew discovered some amazing scientific things to help all of humankind.

I wish I could have been there. I would have created some amazing things too.

Daddy says our people have had a glorious past, and that I have a glorious future. He says I can build and make beautiful things, explore new worlds, and help people who are suffering.

Daddy says there are still plenty of things that need to be invented. He says I can even be a cowgirl if I want to.

I can hardly wait. I want to do something great. Just like the rest of our people.